Postman Pat's
Letters on Ice

Story by **John Cunliffe** *Pictures by* **Celia Berridge**

from the original Television designs by **Ivor Wood**

ANDRE DEUTSCH

First published in 1985 by
André Deutsch Limited
105 Great Russell Street London WC1B 3LJ
Second impression 1988

Text copyright © 1985 by John Cunliffe
Illustrations copyright © 1985 by Celia Berridge and
Woodland Animations Limited

Typeset by Kalligraphics Limited
Printed in Great Britain by Cambus Litho, East Kilbride, Scotland

ISBN 0 233 97766 X

Greendale was having a hard winter, and there had been still more snow in the night. It was icy as well.

Postman Pat was out on his rounds as usual, but he had to go very carefully.

Sam Waldron was out, too, with his mobile shop.
"Hello, Pat!" called Sam. "Rough weather!"
"Hello, Sam. How is it going?"

"Well . . . I don't think I'll be able to get up to Granny Dryden's with her groceries," said Sam. "I got stuck up there yesterday."
"I'll take them with the letters," said Pat. "My van is good in snow."
"Right-o, Pat, here they are."

Sam handed Pat a box full of groceries: packets of tea, biscuits, butter, bread, flour, bacon, sausages, and a big tin of humbugs.

"That'll keep her going for a while," said Pat.
"Thanks," said Sam. "Mind how you go. Cheerio!"

And Pat was on his way.
　　The van skidded and slithered along the steep road to Granny Dryden's house.

She was very glad to see him, specially when she saw he had her groceries, as well as a letter. Pat called out cheerfully, as he came in, "Good morning!"

"Oh, thank you, Pat, that's lovely," said Granny Dryden. "I'll not starve, now. And the letter will be from that lass of mine, in London. I cannot find my reading-glasses anywhere – would you tell me what she says, Pat?"

"Certainly. Now . . . let's see . . ."

Pat tore the envelope open, and read aloud. "She says . . . 'Dear Mum, just a line to let you know . . .'"

"Speak up, please, Pat," said Granny Dryden, "I can't hear you."

Pat went on . . . "'We'll all be able to come up to Greendale to see you for your birthday. Jim started school this week, and Dad's bought a new car. All well, and hoping you are, too. All our love, Sally and family.'"

"Ee, that's good news. Thanks, Pat. Have a cup of tea?"

"Thank you, Mrs. Dryden. It's just the thing, this cold weather."

Pat enjoyed his cup of strong hot tea. "Well, I'll be on my way, before it starts snowing again. Goodbye!"

"Bye, Pat!"

Pat's next stop was at Ted Glen's workshop.

"Morning Ted!"

"Hello, Pat."

Ted was busy sawing some wood.

Pat went to warm himself by Ted's stove. "That's a grand stove you've got there," he said. "I could do with that in my van. Ooooooh . . . it's lovely."

He had a letter for Ted. "Here's someone writing from a warm place – Australia!"

"It'll be our Bert," said Ted. "It's ages since he's written. That reminds me . . . I found Bert's old skates this morning. I reckon they'll be just about your size, Pat. Do you fancy trying them? They say the tarn's frozen hard."

Pat looked at the skates doubtfully. "Well . . . I don't know," he said. "I'd love to have a go. Is the ice safe? Has anyone checked it?"

Ted laughed, "Yes, Miss Hubbard, of course. Take them, anyway; you never know when they might come in handy, and I've got some of my own."

"Thanks, Ted. Cheerio!"

Pat was off again, along the snowy roads. The wind was blowing the snow into drifts, deeper and deeper. Soon, Pat had to stop. The road was blocked with a huge drift of snow. Pat thought he would never get through with his letters now.

Then he looked across to the lake, and saw someone gliding along on the ice. That gave Pat an idea.

"It's worth trying, Jess. I can take a short cut across the lake."

It was George Lancaster, out skating.

"Come on, Pat," he called, "it's lovely."

"You stay here, Jess, and mind the van," said Pat. "I'll just put these skates on."

The skates were a good fit. Pat laced them up firmly, got his bag of letters, and walked carefully out on to the ice.

"Here we go!"

What a time Pat had! He had not skated for years. He toppled and teetered, and nearly fell over, many a time; he went whirling round in circles; he just missed a tree, then had to grab a branch to stop himself.

Somehow, he skated across the lake. Charlie Pringle looked over the wall, and spotted him.

"Hello, Pat," he called. He was very surprised to see Pat arriving on the ice, instead of in his van.

"Hello, Charlie," said Pat. "Special ice-delivery today."

He handed the letters over the wall.
   "Thank you," said Charlie. "Good skating!"

Pat whizzed off again. George Lancaster was still on the ice. He did get a surprise when Pat shot by with a letter for him. Mrs. Thompson was out for a spin, too.

When Pat tried to spin round on the ice, he fell down with a bump.

"Hello, Pat," said Mrs. Thompson, "are you all right? What are you doing down there?"

"Yes, I'm all right," said Pat, and gave her some letters.

"Look at Jess," said Mrs. Thompson.

Jess had come to try his paws at skating. Poor Jess, his paws went in all directions at once.

"Come on, Jess," said Pat, "that's enough skating for today. We'll go back on wheels."

Pat backed his van out of the snow drift, and went on his way.

When Pat arrived at the school, there was no one there: they were all snowed-up at home. But they had left a snowman to wait for Pat. Pat had an old envelope in his pocket, so he addressed it to the snowman – Mr. Snowman, The Drift, Greendale School – and tucked it under the snowman's arm. Then the school door opened; it wasn't empty after all!

"Who's that?" said Pat.

It was Ted Glen and Miss Hubbard.

"Hello, Pat," said Miss Hubbard, "have you seen my bike? The snow must have buried it. We'll have to find it – come on!"

They all searched in the deep snow. Pat thought he saw a handlebar sticking out of the snow, but it was only an old kettle. They found the bike at last, and brushed the snow off it.

"Just in time for choir-practice," said Miss Hubbard. "I'll be off now."

Pat opened the gate for her.

"Thank you, Pat. Goodbye!"

"Bye, Miss Hubbard!"

"Nothing stops her, does it?" said Ted.

"See you in church on Sunday," called Miss Hubbard, as she wobbled off along the snowy road.

Pat could hear Jess, miaowing from the van.

"Coming, Jess," he said. "Time to go home." Jess didn't like the cold weather.

"Cheer up, Jess," said Pat. "This snow can't last forever."